Screamin Calhoun

TOMBSTONES
Volume 2
The Graves

13-Digit ISBN 978-1530854523

Printed in the United States of America

The characters and events in this book are fictitious. Any similarity to real persons, living, dead, or undead is coincidental and not intended by the author.

Living in constant fear and loss of sleep is intended by the author.

Tombstonesbooks.com 2016

The Graves

Screamin Calhoun

TOMBSTONES VOL. 2
THE GRAVES
Screamin Calhoun

Chapter 1

It was the middle of the summer when my family and I moved into our new house next to the dead people. Well, they weren't exactly next door; they were in our backyard. Let me explain. You see, at first it was just two graves, but by the time I figured out...okay, wait a second, I'll start from the beginning so this will make sense.

My parents had this crazy idea that we needed more open space and fresh air. So they dragged my brothers and me out of our comfortable suburban neighborhood and away from my school, my friends, and—worst of all—the mall. My brothers were actually excited about the move. Devin was ten, and Shane was eight, and they were each other's best friend. Having a house on five acres of unexplored land was a dream come true for them.

For me, it was a completely different story. I had been forced to leave my entire social life behind and move to the middle of nowhere. There couldn't be another twelve-year-old girl around for ten miles. Thankfully my dad assured me that we had television and an Internet connection. What else was I supposed to do in the middle of the woods?

After about a three-hour drive, we finally made the turn onto our new street. Cypress Creek Road was three or four miles of twisting, turning asphalt where we passed far more cows than we did houses. And the farther we drove, the more dilapidated the houses became. Many of the houses had obviously not been lived in for decades. Windows were broken, porches collapsed, and one even had the door missing. Finally, the winding stretch of pavement brought us to the bottom of our long dirt driveway.

A traditional yellow farmhouse surrounded by several tall trees stood at the top of a steep hill. I had to admit, our new home was really pretty. There was a front porch that was painted white, which even had a swing on it. The entire family tumbled out of the minivan, and my brothers immediately sprinted to the side of the house where a tire swing hung on an old scraggly tree. I did not share their enthusiasm.

My parents and I stepped up onto the front porch and went over to the railing to watch them. Seeing the amazing scenery around us only made me feel farther away from my perfect life in my old neighborhood.

"You know, Katie," my father began, "you'll meet a lot of new friends at your new school. I really think you'll like it here if you give it a chance."

"I know, Dad," I said. "It really is beautiful. I just miss my friends, that's all."

"Aw, honey, we'll stay in touch with them. I promise," my mom said as she put her arm around me. "And just wait until you see the inside. It's really neat!"

Just then Devin and Shane came running up to the front of the house screaming and yelling. They looked terrified.

"Mom! Dad! Come and look! We found some dead people!"

Chapter 2
THE GRAVES

"Oh, yeah, I kind of forgot to tell you about the previous owners, didn't I?" said my father with a grin on his face.

"Dead people? What are you talking about?" I asked.

"Well, let's go take a look," my dad said as he stepped down off of the porch.

Devin and Shane ran ahead at top speed back around the side of the house. I was totally confused.

"What the heck are you talking about?" I called to my father. But he ignored me and kept walking.

Turning the corner, I saw them. Just past the old crooked tree with the tire swing were two gravestones.

The boys were already down on their knees, trying to read the inscriptions.

"These are awesome! This one is from 1910," Shane yelled.

"We really do have dead people on the side of our house?" I asked.

"Yep, we sure do," my father said. "And we didn't even have to pay extra for them!"

There were two tombstones side by side. One was grey and the other, which was much smaller, was white.

I walked up to them to get a closer look. On the largest tombstone was inscribed:

Frank H Brown
Feb 26, 1825 – Jul 3, 1910

The gravestone next to it stood only about a foot high. It read:

Mary Mabel Carson
July 3rd, 1909 – July 2nd, 1910

"This one was just a baby," I said. "That's why it's so small."

I was fascinated. I loved history. All of the books I read were about the early settlers and their lives. Now I was living on land that had its *own* history. Finally I had found something that excited me about our new house.

"Daddy, who were these people? Did they live here?" I asked.

"I have no idea," said my dad. "They're probably family members from back when this was a farm. All I know is that we had to build the house over there because they couldn't be moved. I'm sure they will be glad to tell you themselves when their ghosts appear at midnight."

"Midnight! What are you talking about?" Shane said as he jerked around towards my father.

My mom glared at my dad, "Oh, stop it, Rob. You're going to make it so he can't sleep." She turned back to Shane and said, "Honey, your dad's just fooling around. There are no such things as ghosts."

"Yeah," I said. "And as for those ghosts that are real, they usually wouldn't do anything to hurt you. As long as you don't stand on their graves."

Devin's and Shane's eyes became as wide as quarters. Slowly, they both turned their heads toward the tombstones and then down to their feet. Devin was standing on Frank, and Shane was standing on Mary Mabel.

They quickly glanced up at each other and froze. Then they screamed and ran to the house, their arms waving wildly over their heads like a bunch of fools.

My father and I burst into laughter and gave each other a high five.

"Oh, great. Thanks a lot," my mom said. "I can see I'm going to have a long night tonight."

"Good one," Dad said, laughing. "We'll both be able to tease them about this for years! Now that's something to look forward to."

"Yeah, you both are real mature," my mother said as she walked toward the house. My dad put his arm around me, and we followed.

"C'mon," he said. "Let's go inside and see if there are any other dead bodies still lying around."

I was excited. I knew that I had to find the real story behind the tombstones. The graves were a mystery that begged to be solved, and I vowed I would spend the summer doing just that.

Chapter 3
THE GRAVES

The inside of the house was absolutely beautiful. I started looking around the first floor, but my brothers couldn't wait to see their bedroom. As soon as we were in sight of the stairs, they raced ahead, pushing and shoving each other to be the first to the top.

I followed with Mom and Dad at a more civilized pace.

My father called the boys back, "Slow down, cowpokes, wait a second. Let us catch up, and I'll give you the tour."

The first room we came to was mine. It was a fairly good size, even a little bigger than my old one.

There were only two windows, and they overlooked the backyard and the woods. Although the room wasn't the biggest, it was right next to the bathroom, which made it perfect for me.

At the end of the hall, we finally came to the boys' room. It was gigantic. The room stretched from one side of the house to the other and had windows on the front, back, and several on the sides.

I had to admit I was feeling more than a little jealous. I knew the reason they had the bigger room was because they were sharing it, but I was older after all.

My brothers ran around like a bunch of gorillas.

"Man, we could play a basketball game in here!" Devin shouted.

"Uh-oh, Devin, come look at this," Shane said, looking out of one of the side windows.

Just below the window sat the two gravestones and the scraggly willow tree.

"Aw, man, you're sleeping on that side of the room," Devin said.

"No way!" Shane hollered.

"Hey, guys," I said. "Why don't you both put your beds on this side of the room? You can see for miles from over here."

Just then, something caught my attention as I looked out of the front window. I squinted and leaned forward just a bit.

"Whoa, whose freaky house is that?" I said.

My parents walked over, and Devin and Shane pushed in front of them. Through the trees, we could see a spooky, old abandoned house just across the road.

It looked like it was at least a hundred years old and had not been taken care of at all. Many of the shingles on the roof were missing, and several of the shutters hung precariously by a single nail. There was no way of telling what the original color of the house was because it hadn't been painted in decades. There was no front yard to speak of because weeds and vines had overtaken the entire area, all except a barely worn path leading to the porch.

Then I noticed something even weirder.

"Look, there are no windows," I said.

"Hey, you're right," my dad said. "Well, actually, there used to be, but they've been bricked over. That's strange; usually people use plywood to cover the windows of an abandoned house to keep the rain and the animals out. Bricks seem kind of permanent and a bit overkill. Whoever took the time to do that didn't want anything to get into there...ever."

Devin backed away from the window. "Man, that's scary looking," he said.

"Aw, guys, you don't have to worry," I said. "Whatever ghosts live in there probably can't get out anyway. I'm sure that's why they had to brick up the windows. It should hold unless you make too much noise and irritate them." Then I turned to my dad and winked.

Devin and Shane stood motionless and stared out the window. My mom turned to me and said, "Oh, Katie, would you stop it?" Then she looked back at the boys, "Now, boys, you know there are no such things as..."

"Aaaaaaaahhhhhhhhhhhhh!" my brothers screamed as they stared wide-eyed at the haunted house.

The front door of the old house had opened slowly. An old man with a beard and a cowboy hat had stepped out onto the front porch. He looked around slowly and then stared straight up at our window. He had seen us all watching him!

I jumped backwards from the window to keep from being seen, but it was too late.

"Somebody actually lives in there? Oooooh, creepy," I said, wiggling my fingers at Devin and Shane.

The boys backed away from the window that faced the haunted house while glancing over their shoulders at the window overlooking the graves. There was absolutely no place in the room that they would be safe from being eaten. After about six backward steps, they took off running down the hallway, screaming their heads off.

Chapter 4
THE GRAVES

A few hours later, the moving van arrived.
By evening, the huge truck had been unloaded and our
house was filled with boxes.

The graves had turned out to be my good
fortune. With my assistance, my brothers had been so
freaked out by both the tombstones and the old man
across the street that they refused to stay in the big
bedroom and insisted on switching with me. They
figured that since the room was the closest to the
graves, the ghost of Mary Mabel would claim it as her
own.

Instead, they wanted to share one of the tiny
rooms in the middle of the house to be as far away from

any window as possible. It had worked out perfectly. I managed to get the big room all to myself. I had more than enough room to hold all of my things, which were, of course, stacked in brown boxes in every corner.

Only a few things were actually set up, all of the necessities. My bed was in the middle with my yellow ducky quilt. I loved anything yellow. My iPod and speakers were set up on my nightstand. Because the room was so huge, I convinced my parents to let me have the sleep sofa that was originally supposed to be in the basement. It was the perfect sleepover room...if I ever met another friend.

But the first thing that I set up was my desk and laptop, which was by far my most important possession. I loved my computer, and now it was my only connection to my social life back home.

I spent the rest of the night listening to music and texting with my old friends. By ten o'clock, everyone had said everything possible there was to say, so I put away my phone and collapsed onto my bed. The only light in the room was a lamp still sitting on the floor. The window shades were not put up yet, so when I turned off the lamp, the ceiling was covered with a web of shadows emanating from the outside moonlight. I lay there for a while, lost in thought as the dark forms danced above me.

With my mind focused on the movement of the ceiling, I knew that sleep was a long way off. I rolled off the bed and stood at the window overlooking the tombstones.

The night had gotten very dark. There were no streetlights or other houses nearby to brighten the scenery. Only the moonlight and the stars illuminated the outside world.

In this light, the gnarled willow tree just outside my window was especially eerie looking. The knots in the twisted trunk created dark, recessed shadows. The long, flowing branches drifting in the wind gave the impression that the tree was moving on its own.

Everything was covered with a veil of blackness except for the gravestones. The moon seemed to shine on the white marble and nothing else. The glow was so noticeable that they appeared to be lit from the inside. The branches of the tree looked as if they were clawing the ground, trying to scratch the dirt from the graves.

The moonlight shining through the leaves made the shadows and deep recesses of the gnarly trunk swirl. As I looked closer, the dark, malignant spots became ugly, distorted faces. I imagined that the tree contained the trapped souls of the graves trying to escape.

The wind blew harder, and the dangling limbs were stretching out, coming closer to where I stood at the bedroom window. But I couldn't take my eyes from the trunk. Something inside seemed to be moving, struggling to be free from the ancient bark.

And then, with a loud crash, a huge branch fell from the tree and landed on Mary Mabel's grave. I let out a quick scream and jumped back from the window.

Whoa! That was freaky, I thought. *And how long have I been staring out of that window anyway?* I turned and looked at the clock on my nightstand. It read 1:15 a.m. I had been standing there for almost three hours! I closed the curtain and quickly stepped backwards. I took two steps and leaped onto my bed and curled up under the covers. In an effort to clear my head, I tried to think about my previous life.

But I couldn't get the image of the haunted tree out of my mind. The imagined faces in the trunk continued to flash in my mind.

Geez, what's wrong with me? I thought. *I'm as wimpy as my brothers. It's only a tree, after all.*

I rolled over onto my other side and tried to find sleep.

Just a tree, I thought. *Yeah, a tree with tortured souls trapped inside!*

Then I remembered what Shane had said: "Mary Mabel would make this room hers."

It was going to be a long night.

Chapter 5
THE GRAVES

The next morning was Saturday, and I awoke much earlier than usual. The excitement of being in a new home, possibly even a haunted one, made it difficult to sleep.

My parents were already awake and had begun the never-ending process of unpacking boxes from the move. I walked into the kitchen, where my mom was knee-deep in cardboard, trying to figure out where everything would go.

"So, what do we have around here for breakfast?" I asked jokingly.

"That's a good question," she said. "Until I get to the store, we really don't have many choices. There's a box on the counter with some cereal, but we don't have any milk."

"Oh, great, dry Chocolate Poofs," I said. I looked in the refrigerator, hoping to find something decent, but it was completely empty.

"Okay, relax," said my mom. "There's a little store about a mile down the road. I'll run down there and get a few of the basics."

"There's a store around here? Oooo, let me go. I'll ride my bike!"

After a few minutes of arguing about getting lost, hit by a car, talking to strangers, and possible natural disasters, she finally said the magic words, "Go ask your dad."

I knew my dad would let me go. He was always trying to get me to be more adventurous and encouraged me to do things on my own. As I expected, ten minutes later, I had dug out my bike from the garage and was headed down the driveway with some money and a grocery list.

At the bottom of the hill, through the trees, I could see the old abandoned house. It was much scarier up close, and everything around it seemed eerily quiet. I sped around the corner, fearing the old man would be somewhere outside. I tore down the empty road, all the while with the hair standing up on the back of my neck, feeling that I was being watched.

McCord's General Store was easy to find because it was right on Cypress Creek Road. I passed only three or four houses and only saw one car during the entire mile ride. It felt fantastic to have the freedom to explore my new town all on my own.

I pulled into the gravel parking area of the old brown building and leaned my bike against the side of the store. An old grey dog lay next to the wooden screen door. I took a few steps closer, and it wagged its tail without bothering to get up or even lift its head.

The clang of the bells surprised me when I pulled the door open, announcing my arrival to the completely empty store. McCord's was not big at all. There was a counter with an antique cash register to the right and only three aisles of shelves on the left.

A few seconds later, a girl came out of the back room. She had red hair and freckles and looked about my age. I must have looked surprised, as I figured some ninety-year-old man in overalls would be the proprietor. She also seemed a bit startled to see me.

"Hi! Can I help you?" she asked.

"Oh, I'm just here to pick up a few things for breakfast," I said, pulling out the list from my pocket.

"You mean you're not just passing through?" she asked.

I was unsure of how to answer the question. "Um, no, I just moved in up the road."

"Really! You live here?" she said in amazement. "Oh, this is great! There's never been another girl around. I'm Lauren. What's your name?"

"I'm Katie," I said a little too softly.

"Maybe we could hang out this afternoon," said Lauren. "I could show you around. I get off work in about an hour."

"You actually work here?" I asked. "How old are you?"

"I'm only twelve, but this is my family's store. My grandma used to run it, but now my dad does, and I help out sometimes."

"That's pretty cool. Sure, let's do something later. What time do you want me to come by?" I asked.

"Why don't I come by your house when I am finished here?" said Lauren. "I'd love to see your house."

I told Lauren where I lived and bought the groceries I had come for. After a short while, I was back on my bike and pedaling home at top speed. It was exciting to have a new friend. I couldn't wait to tell my parents.

It felt neat to walk into the kitchen with breakfast for the family. The freedom to explore was something new to me. I ate my Chocolate Poofs with my milk that I was so proud of and waited for Lauren to arrive. She seemed so friendly and outgoing. I knew we would get along perfectly, but I was still nervous.

A few hours later, the doorbell finally rang. I hopped down the steps and then tried to walk a little slower so as not to appear overly anxious. I didn't want to seem desperate to have a friend, although inside I had butterflies in my stomach.

"Hi, how are you?" I said. "Did you find the house okay?"

"Around here?" she laughed. "Everyplace is easy to find around here. Wow! This place is beautiful. I have never seen a new house in this town...ever. Everything is a gazillion years old."

"Yeah, um, thanks. Do you want to come up and see my room?" I asked. "Unfortunately, I still have a lot of unpacking to do."

"Sure, let's go," Lauren said cheerfully.

I led her up the stairs and down to the end of the hallway.

"Wow, look how big your room is! You have so much space."

"Yeah, there will be even more just as soon as I get all these boxes unpacked," I said.

"Well, let's do it right now!" Lauren hollered as she ripped the tape off of the closest box.

"Nah, you didn't come here to unpack boxes. Why don't we go for a walk or something?"

"Aw, don't be silly. Anyway, it'll give me a chance to see all of your stuff," she said, laughing. "I'm kind of nosey."

We spent the next hour or so getting my room organized. Lauren was very easy to talk to because she was so outgoing. She seemed to take an interest in just about everything we took out of a box. In no time at all, my room had been transformed from a mere storage bin to a beautiful bedroom.

"Look at this place," Lauren said. "You could have your own party in here."

"Thanks to you," I said. "These boxes would probably have been here another month from now without your help."

"And look at this view you have from here," said Lauren as she walked over to the window on the side of the house. "You can see half the county."

Suddenly, Lauren let out a scream.

"Oh, man, there's a graveyard down there," she said, staring wide-eyed at the tombstones.

"Oh, yeah, isn't it freaky?" I said.

"Freaky? It's like a horror movie or something! Who are they?"

"I don't know, but they've been dead for over a hundred years."

"Oh, I know who they are!" Lauren began. "The story goes that two girls were killed about a hundred years ago by a crazy man right here in this field because they had trespassed on his property. People say that every year, the girls rise from their graves and search for any relatives of the murderer to seek revenge. The problem is that no one knows who the descendants of the crazy man are, so everyone runs around scared every June 24th."

"June 24th? That's today!" I said, staring at Lauren, frozen with fear.

After a brief pause, we each grabbed the other by the arms and screamed at the top of our lungs.

Chapter 6
THE GRAVES

By the time we reached the bottom of the steps, Lauren was almost in tears from laughter. I quickly figured out that she had been joking all along, and I joined her in falling on the floor and giggling.

"Geez, what's so funny?" my father asked as he came through the front door carrying still more boxes.

"Lauren's just telling ghost stories about the graveyard out back," I said. "She really got me good!"

"Whew!" Lauren said, catching her breath and clutching her side. "I really had you going there. C'mon, let's go outside. I'd like to get a closer look at those tombstones."

"All right!" my father yelled after us as we headed out the door. "But no shovels!"

Lauren was so excited she ran ahead of me.

"Wow! You are so lucky. You have your very own ghosts!" she squealed.

"Yeah, isn't it the coolest?"

"Do you know who they are?" she asked.

"No. I asked my parents, and even the builders have no idea," I said, shrugging my shoulders.

"Look, this one was just a baby," said Lauren. "Look how small the tombstone is."

"Yeah, that's really sad," I said. "She died just before her first birthday."

"Hey, look at this," said Lauren. "The two of them died just one day apart. See, July 2nd, 1910, and July 3rd, 1910. I wonder what the story behind that is."

"I don't know, but I am dying to find out," I said.

"Oooo, this is great! Our very own mystery," said Lauren. She was hopping up and down, clapping her hands together. From a distance, she must have looked very strange jumping and cheering at someone's gravestone. "I bet we could go to the town library and find out everything. C'mon, let's go now! The library is right near my house."

Her excitement was contagious. It was neat to have something undiscovered right here in my own backyard.

"I can't believe that you are as excited about this as I am," I said. "I thought I would be the only nerd around here."

"Are you crazy?" said Lauren. "I love this kind of stuff. Besides, what else would I be doing anyway? If you haven't noticed, this place is dead."

"Dead…no pun intended, huh?" I said, laughing. "Let's go see if my dad can give us a ride."

"Aw, c'mon, city girl. Don't you have a bike?" Lauren chided. "We could even walk. It's only a couple of miles from here."

"I guess so," I said with a slight hesitation. "Let me go ask my dad."

As we turned to go back in the house, something caught my eye across the road. I turned and looked down the hill. Lauren turned her head in the same direction.

Standing on his front porch was the old man. He remained there motionless, glaring at us with a horribly mean scowl. He looked disturbed.

"Oh, no," I said in a very low voice. "He must have seen you dancing around on the grave!"

Chapter 7
THE GRAVES

"Oh my goodness! Who is that crazy old man?" Lauren asked breathlessly as we slammed the door behind us, giggling nervously.

"That's the town axe murderer, that's who that is! The one you told me about," I answered. "I think he's five hundred years old or something."

"How long do you think he has been watching us?"

"Who knows?" I answered. "But he sure is freaking me out!"

We went directly to the window and peaked out from behind the curtain, but he had vanished.

"Well, your house certainly has all of the excitement you'll ever need...a couple of ghosts and an axe murderer. Geez, you're lucky!" Lauren said, laughing.

A few minutes later, we were headed down my driveway on our hike to the library. At the bottom, just past the trees, stood the old man's house.

"Man, that's a scary-looking place," Lauren said.

"Tell me about it," I muttered.

We walked quietly, hoping not to be seen, but it felt as if the house were watching us. Surely the old man couldn't have been looking because there were no windows. We reached the end of the driveway and then turned quickly onto Cypress Creek Road towards town.

But Lauren didn't turn.

"Hold on, Katie. I have to make a quick stop," she said.

She was walking straight across the road, directly to the axe murderer's house!

"Lauren," I whispered as loudly as I could. "What are you doing?"

"Oh, just being neighborly," she responded cheerfully. "And doing a little research," she said with a wink.

"You're crazy! Come back here!"

But it was no use. She was already on the first step as she waved for me to come along. Begrudgingly, I followed.

The old steps creaked and groaned, loudly announcing our visit long before we reached the door. I felt like I would jump out of my skin, but Lauren stepped confidently to the front door and knocked.

A moment later, we heard a gruff shout of, "Who's there!" from the inside. It was less of a question and more of a demand.

"Um...it's....it's two of your neighbors," Lauren said, her voice quivering slightly.

I couldn't believe we were standing on the porch. I thought for sure that he would open the door carrying a shotgun and start yelling at us.

There was a pause that lasted an eternity, and then we heard the deadbolt lock slide open. That was followed by another three or four locks and what seemed like thick chains being removed. It was like trying to enter a safe!

The door opened a crack, and the old man peered out, his eyes squinting from the sunlight. When he saw two nervous girls on the porch, his face softened, and he opened the door fully.

"Well, hey there, girls. What brings y'all over here?"

His voice was rough, as expected, but he didn't seem nearly as scary. In fact, he appeared almost welcoming.

"Um, hi," Lauren said meekly. "I'm Lauren, and I live just down the road, and this is my friend Katie who just moved in up on the hill."

I raised my hand slightly above my shoulder and very tentatively said, "Hi." I felt like a complete moron.

"We thought we would stop by and introduce ourselves," added Lauren.

"Well, pleasure to make your acquaintance, ladies. I don't get visitors too often. Matter of fact...never! I'm Douglas Miller," he said, reaching out to shake our hands. "But I guess you should call me Mr. Miller since I'm a couple hundred years older than the two of you."

He couldn't bring himself to smile, but he was still amazingly friendly. Surprisingly, once he began speaking, he didn't want to stop.

"I've lived here for ninety-five years, blah, blah, blah. Born and raised right in this same here spot, blah, blah, blah. And you know what's funny? Since y'all built that there house, you're the first neighbors I've ever had. For decades, this place was the only house on the entire road, blah, blah, blah. Seemed folks were afraid of what happened back in 1910."

I asked the obvious question: "What happened back in 1910?"

"They didn't tell you nothin' bout dem graves up on your property?"

"No, sir," I answered. "All we know was that one was an old man and the other was a little baby."

"But we're really interested in finding out more," Lauren added. "I noticed they died just one day apart."

"So you don't know about the others?" Mr. Miller asked.

"Others?" I said. "What...others?"

Chapter 8
THE GRAVES

"Oh, there's a whole mess of 'em up on your property," said Mr. Miller.

"We've seen the two gravestones up by the big tree there, but where are the others?" I asked.

"Well, you won't find the others. There ain't no markings for them. They weren't meant to be found," he said, leaning closer to us and lowering his voice.

"What do you mean?" I asked, bubbling over with excitement. "Are they a secret or something? I can't wait to go searching for them!"

Then a noticeable change came over Old Man Miller. Suddenly, he wasn't as eager to talk. His face became both concerned and irritated.

"Now, it ain't no secret!" he barked. "Just some stupid legend. You two just make sure you treat dem graves with respect! And don't go on some harebrained treasure hunt."

He had a crazed look about him, almost as if he were becoming a different person. His eyes were darting back and forth, and he appeared very nervous, almost frightened.

We definitely no longer seemed welcome, and it was clear that this conversation was now over. I instinctively took a step backwards to allow for a quick retreat. Even Lauren didn't seem like talking much.

"Yes, sir, we will...I mean we won't...um...yes, sir," she said meekly.

"See to it!" he said, turning his back to us and opening his screen door. He was obviously finished with this conversation and wanted us to leave.

"Okay, it was nice meeting..." Lauren said, but the door had closed abruptly before Lauren had a chance to complete her sentence. Then we heard the series of locks being closed one after the other.

Lauren turned to me with a comical look on her face and said in a low voice, "Let's get out of here." We quickly hopped down the steps and dashed across the road.

"What was all that about?" I asked.

"I don't know, but we obviously did something wrong," said Lauren.

"I don't think we did anything wrong. I think he just said too much."

"You mean you think that there really are a bunch of secret graves up there?" asked Lauren.

"You saw how upset he was. There's something he doesn't want us to know," I said, looking over Lauren's shoulder at Old Man Miller's house.

"I don't think I want to know either," said Lauren, turning her head to follow my gaze.

"Are you kidding me? I *have* to know now! There is no way I'll ever fall asleep at night unless I find out."

With that, I grabbed Lauren's hand and said, "Now how do we get to the library?"

Chapter 9
THE GRAVES

After about a fifteen-minute walk, we arrived at the town. Directly in front of us was the only traffic light for miles. The town consisted of a single intersection, a few shops and stores, a diner, and at the far end of the block, the library.

The library was a stately building with finely manicured landscaping. The building was not extremely large, but it was obvious that it was the pride of the community. The marble steps, albeit only three, were capped on either side with cement lions, and the double doors had shiny brass handles.

We walked inside, and Lauren followed me to the information desk. I explained that we were looking to do some research on a family burial plot, and the librarian took us to a separate room called the Maryland Archives.

All of the books in this room were very old and extremely boring. I pulled out one that caught my eye entitled <u>Cemetery Inscriptions of Anne Arundel County, Maryland</u>. Inside were listings of cemeteries and family burial plots detailing the writing on the tombstones.

Alphabetically under the C's we found an entry entitled Cypress Creek Road – Brown Plot. The entry stated very plainly:

Gravestones at the Corner of Cypress Creek and Dill Roads

Mary Mabel Carson
Born July 3rd, 1909 Died July 2nd, 1910

Frank H. Brown
Born February 26th, 1825 Died July 3rd, 1910

"That's it?" Lauren said in a whisper. "Where are the other ones?"

"This book only tells us what is listed on the grave markers," I said. "We're looking for graves that might not even have a tombstone at all. Hey, how about this one?"

I pulled out a tall, dark brown leather-bound journal titled <u>Maryland Mortalities 1876-1915</u>.

"Oooooh, that sounds seriously spooky!" said Lauren.

I opened it up, only to be disappointed once again. It was merely an alphabetical listing of everyone who had died in Maryland listing the date and location. This only would have helped us if we had known the names of the other people who had died. I turned to the C's to find Mary Mabel Carson. It was easy to find because someone had already circled it.

"That's weird...someone else was looking her up too?" asked Lauren. The page read...

Callahan, Shaun, 63, died Jan 10, 1914, Baltimore City, gunshot
Callahan, Colin, 75, died Feb 26, 1884, Baltimore City, wrecking ball
Callahan, Daisy, 29, died May 22, 1904, Howard Co, shark attack
Carson, Henry, 42, died Jul 12, 1910, A.A. County, unknown
Carson, Mary, 11 mos., died Jul 2, 1910, A.A. County, influenza
Carson, Mary, 41, died Feb 15, 1896, A.A. County, heart attack
Carson, Thomas, 26, died Jul 12, 1910, A.A. County, unknown
Carson, Wilbur, 71, died Apr 1, 1902, Howard County, lion attack
Carson, Samuel, 54, died Jul 12, 1910, A.A. County, unknown
Casanova, Anna, 68, died Jan 7, 1894, Baltimore City, ill health
Casanova, Florence, died Aug 4, 1903, Calvert Co, electrocution

"Look, Lauren," I said. "It says she died of the flu!"

"Yeah, I heard that people sometimes die of that, usually really old people or young babies."

"That's why my grandma gets a flu shot every year."

"That's a pain in the butt. My family never gets them," I said.

"Actually, it's a pain in the arm," said Lauren, laughing.

"Ouch, I hate needles. I'd rather just go ahead and die," I said.

Then Lauren noticed something in the book.

"Hey, look at these other Carsons," she said. "They all died in the same year."

"Wait a minute," I said. "They all died on the same day, just ten days after Mary Mabel died, and all in Anne Arundel County!"

"These must be the other graves," said Lauren. "But look, they don't know how they died."

I turned to the B's and found the entry for Frank Brown to see if a cause of death was listed. Sure enough, he too had died of influenza.

I knelt down to put the book back on the shelf. As I slid it in, I noticed the book next to it, which read Influenza Shots in Anne Arundel County, Maryland, 1909-1925.

"Hey, look at this one. Maybe this will help," I said.

Again, I turned the pages looking for Frank Brown. He wasn't listed. Then I turned to the C's to find Mary Mabel. There was no listing for her either.

"Well, I guess they didn't get their flu shots," said Lauren. "That would explain it. That's why they died."

"Yeah, but look at the other Carsons listed on the page," I said.

Carson, Henry   Anne Arundel Co. Jul 4, 1910
Carson, Thomas   Anne Arundel Co. Jul 4, 1910
Carson, Samuel   Anne Arundel Co. Jul 4, 1910

The information was right in front of us in black and white, but it didn't seem to make any sense. All of the Carsons who had died on July 12, 1910, were listed. The flu shots had been given just eight days before they had died.

Chapter 10
THE GRAVES

"Okay, so all of these people died from the flu? I guess our mystery is solved," said Lauren. "Boy, that was boring. Let's go get some ice cream or something."

"No, they didn't die from the flu," I said. All of these people had their flu vaccinations. The first two, Mary Mabel and Frank, died from the flu, and that probably convinced the others to go and get their shots. The shots must have worked. Otherwise, the book would have listed the cause of death as 'influenza', not 'unknown'."

"That's a good point, but something happened on July 12, 1910," said Lauren.

"That's the real mystery. That...and where the heck are the bodies?" I said.

"No, the real mystery is what is your favorite kind of ice cream?" asked Lauren.

"Mint chocolate chip, but c'mon, don't you want to figure this out?" I asked.

"They'll still be in their graves tomorrow," said Lauren. "Wherever they are."

"Yeah, but we're here now. Let me at least talk to the librarian. Maybe she can help us."

A few minutes later, the librarian was logging us on to a website, and in no time at all, we were looking at the July 12th, 1910, issue of the Baltimore Sun newspaper.

Several pages back, we found an article on the events that occurred on Cypress Creek Road. It read

Area Quarantined Over Flu Fears

Anne Arundel County – The National Guard and state officials have quarantined Cypress Creek Road, along with all neighboring roads, for fear of a fast-moving influenza epidemic spreading through the area. The quarantine, ordered by the governor, forces all people living in the area to remain in their homes. The National Guard, assisted by the Maryland State Police, has set up outposts surrounding the area to enforce the order.

The only incoming traffic allowed to enter the area are vehicles from the State of Maryland Department of Health. Doctors and emergency workers will be delivering food and administering medicines in order to fight the fast-moving disease.

The problem first attracted public attention when two deaths occurred on consecutive days one week prior. Mary Mable Carson, age 1, and Frank H. Brown, age 63, died of influenza on July 2nd and 3rd, respectively. As a result, county officials, following state emergency procedures for contagious disease breakouts, ordered all residents within a two-mile radius to receive mandatory flu shots.

Several residents complained because the newly developed treatment has not been fully tested. However, officials made the decision to make the flu shots mandatory for the residents because of the greater risk of the deadly virus spreading to an uncontrollable metropolitan area. All residents received the injection on July 4th.

It is not clear why the National Guard has been called in to enforce the quarantine order issued eight days after the shots were given. When asked for comment, Randall Shaull, spokesperson for the Department of Health, said, "It is believed that the batch of flu vaccine given was not effective against this particular strain of the disease."

When asked to elaborate on the symptoms of the individuals, Mr. Shaull stated that all other information was classified and would be released at a later date.

"Well, that certainly confirms Old Man Miller's story about a bunch of people being buried at your house," said Lauren.

"It sure does," I said. "But why would any of that information be classified?" I said. "I mean, if it's just the flu, what's so top secret about that?"

"Maybe it wasn't just the flu," said Lauren. "It sounds a whole lot scarier than that."

Chapter 11
THE GRAVES

I couldn't wait to tell my parents. Lauren and I rushed home. Somewhere on our five acres of property was the answer to a mystery that was over one hundred years old!

When we arrived at my house, Devin and Shane were leaving the garage with their wagon full of shovels and buckets.

"We found the coolest place!" Shane yelled. "You have to come see it!"

We followed them to the edge of the woods behind our house. At that point, they had to leave the wagon behind because the vines and bushes were so overgrown. The boys grabbed the shovels and carried them by hand.

For much of the hike, our feet never actually touched the ground. The trees were so thick and numerous that we were constantly climbing over or walking along fallen tree trunks.

"Wait until you see this place," Devin said. "It's awesome!"

It was a slow-moving process. We were always either climbing over or under something. Although we had walked for nearly ten minutes, we had probably only traveled a few hundred yards.

My brothers were about fifteen feet in front of Lauren and me, and it was difficult to keep up. Because they were smaller, they could navigate the branches with ease like a couple of monkeys.

"Where are you taking us?" I hollered

"You'll see!" they yelled back. "It's just ahead!"

We came across the top of a giant fallen tree. The boys were already standing on top of the massive trunk, yelling back at us, "Come on, slow pokes, you're almost there!"

I climbed up onto the trunk of the tree, which was at least five feet off of the ground. It was wide enough that my brothers could run across it quickly without fear of falling off. I traveled much slower than they did and had to crawl along it like a baby to reach the end.

When we reached the base, I realized that the entire root system of the tree had been ripped from the ground. Finally, I stood up by holding onto one of the big roots and saw what had excited my brothers so thoroughly.

Beyond the fallen tree, the dense, wooded thicket abruptly vanished. In front of us was a large patch of dirt about thirty feet across. It was like nothing had been able to grow in this spot. The clearing was inaccessible by any other route because it was surrounded by a wall of leaves, branches, and tree trunks.

The boys tossed their shovels onto the ground and hopped down into the clearing. Lauren and I climbed down more cautiously.

"Isn't this neat?" Devin said.

"Yeah, we've got our own hideout," said Shane. No one will ever find this place!"

It was quite a fort. Everything around us was green. The vines, trees, and bushes were in full bloom.

But for some reason, in this one area, nothing grew, not even a single blade of grass or a weed. The ground looked completely dead.

Chapter 12
THE GRAVES

"You're right," I said. "This is amazing. But there's only one thing I don't understand. What's up with the shovels?"

"Look over here," said Devin as he walked back over to the base of the uprooted tree. "There's a bunch of old bricks under the tree stump. We're gonna dig 'em up and use them to build walls."

Under the huge ball of roots that had been torn out of the ground, twenty or thirty unearthed bricks were visible. Some were loose and had been randomly strewn about from the tree falling. However, most were placed neatly side by side, as if a patio or floor had been constructed in this spot.

The boys started moving the bricks. At first they were easy to pick up because several of them were just lying on the ground. But the bricks that were still in place were more difficult to unearth. They were covered with a layer of dirt three inches deep that had accumulated over many years.

By using the shovels, Shane was able to pry one of the bricks loose with ease. Devin reached down and picked it up, only to discover a layer of old wood underneath.

The boys were even more excited.

"Oh, wow!" said Devin. "We can have brick walls and a wood floor! Come on, let's dig up the rest!"

For the next half hour, Shane dug up the bricks, Devin shoveled the loose dirt away, and Lauren and I put the bricks in a pile.

In the middle of the clearing, we made another strange discovery. At first it looked like we had found a piece of metal that was nailed into the wood. Then, as more dirt and bricks were cleared away, we began to realize that we had found something more important.

There were several metal pieces. And the pieces were, in fact, the hinges of a door.

"What the heck is this?" Lauren said.

"A secret passageway or something," said Shane.

"Come on," said Devin. "Clear the rest of it off so we can open it up! There's probably treasure buried under there!"

Lauren and I took the shovels to speed things along. We dug furiously for the next few minutes, and very shortly, we had uncovered the entire door.

It was very large, about four feet wide and six feet long. On the opposite side, a very old, rusted padlock was attached. It was the kind that required a key, and the key hole was completely filled with dirt.

Then I noticed something else odd.

"Look, there's no door handle," I said. "How are we going to get this thing open?"

"What about the lock?" asked Lauren. "I think that might be our first problem."

Devin reached over and grabbed the large metal shovel from my hands.

"Stand back," he commanded. "I think I can manage that."

He raised the heavy shovel above his head and brought it down with a loud THUMP! Unfortunately, it landed right on the wood and missed the old metal lock completely.

"Strike one!" yelled Shane. "Here, let me have a try," he said, yanking the shovel out of Devin's hands.

Shane's aim was much better, but his strength was not. The shovel came down directly on the lock, but it didn't break.

"All right, let a woman show you how it's done," I said.

I picked up the shovel and, using the sharp edge instead of the flat part, thrust it down powerfully into the center of the lock. The rusted antique broke into two pieces and fell away from the door as all of us cheered with delight.

"All right, Lauren," I said. "Grab that other shovel, and let's pry this baby open! We're gonna be rich!"

Chapter 13
THE GRAVES

Lauren and I each took a shovel and wedged it into the crack of the door. Devin stood on one side, and Shane stood on the other, each with a large stick ready to slide under the door once we got it open a few inches.

"All right, get ready," Lauren said. "On three we'll lift it up, and you guys shove the branches in. One...two...THREE!"

We pushed down hard on the shovels, and the door came up a few inches. It was just enough for Shane to get a branch wedged into the opening.

A burst of stale air poured out of the small crack on all sides, releasing a cloud of greenish dust all around us. Lauren and I dropped our shovels, and all four of us began coughing and wheezing from the noxious fumes. The cloud of gas burned my eyes, and I ran to the edge of the clearing, fighting for breath.

Gagging and eyes watering, I looked back to the trapdoor. The billowing dust was neon green and was rising slowly above the trees. After a few moments, the cloud had dissipated, and I could start to breathe normally again.

"Ewww!" I said. "What the heck was that?"

"I don't know, some sort of decades-old gas," said Lauren.

"Yeah, well, whoever smelt it dealt it!" said Devin in his never-ending quest for the perfect bathroom joke.

"Yeah, yeah, real funny," I said, trying to discourage him from embarrassing me any further.   But Shane was already rolling on the ground laughing. It didn't take a lot to amuse these two.

"All right, all right," I said. "Come on, let's see what's inside."

With the stick propping it open, we were able to grip the edges of the door. The huge slab of wood creaked and groaned as the rusted hinges resisted any movement. The door felt like it were made of cement, and it took all four of us to open it completely.

Once it was opened fully, we let it fall backwards onto the ground. The sound of the door hitting the dirt was like thunder. Leaves scattered with the wind from the door's impact, and birds noisily flew from the surrounding trees.

The four of us stood above the opening. I had expected to see a treasure chest, or at least some stairs leading to an underground cave. But all we saw was a dark hole. It was deep enough that we couldn't see to the bottom. Because of the dense trees that surrounded the clearing, there was not enough sunlight to illuminate the inside.

We lay on our stomachs and hung our heads over the doorway, but it was of no use. I could tell that there was something down there from outlines and shadows, but couldn't make out specific objects.

As I got to my feet, I noticed the back of the door. There were what looked like scratches, some of them deep gouges. Splinters jutted outward like stalagmites in a cave. Many spots were discolored with dark-brown disgusting stains.

The four of us examined it, wondering what could have caused this damage. Lauren thought that the scratches were done purposefully, with a rock or a tool.

"It looks like an animal was scratching on it to me," I said. "Like something was trying to get out. Don't those stains look like old, dried blood?"

"Awww, gross!" cried Shane.

"Well, whatever it was is probably still down there," said Lauren. "Let's get some flashlights and a rope."

"A rope? I'm not going down there," I said.

"Of course not," said Lauren. "The boys will. They're lighter and can fit easier. And they are much better climbers."

"No way!" they hollered.

"All right, forget the rope then," she said. "Go get a couple of flashlights, and let's at least see how deep this thing is."

My brothers eagerly volunteered to run off into the woods, rather than stand guard by the dark open hole.

Lauren and I waited in the clearing for the boys to return, wondering if our discovery was buried treasure...or something else.

Chapter 14
THE GRAVES

Ten minutes later, Devin and Shane jumped off
the giant fallen tree and landed in the clearing, each
carrying a flashlight. The four of us went directly over to
the trapdoor and got down on our knees for a closer
look.

Devin switched his flashlight on and, to our
horror, Lauren and I knew immediately what we had
found.

In the hole, which looked to be about ten feet
deep, were the bodies we were searching for. But this
wasn't just a big grave. This was a gigantic hole in the
ground. It was more of a burial room. We were looking
directly at dead bodies!

And the skeletons weren't laid side by side as would be expected. Some of them lay on top of the others in a heap. Others sat upright along the sides. There must have been fifteen bodies, all randomly scattered throughout the hole.

But the strangest part of the scene was the green dust that covered all the bodies. It seemed to grow on them like a fungus. It gave the skeletons a novelty type of appearance like Halloween decorations purchased from a store.

Devin and Shane stared in wide-eyed silence at the grotesque discovery.

"We found it!" I yelled. "We found the others!"

"I can't believe it!" said Lauren. "But I still don't understand *what* we've found. These aren't graves!"

"Found what?" Devin asked.

"Yeah, what do you mean by 'others'?" asked Shane.

"Lauren and I were talking to the old man across the street and—"

"You saw the old man?" screamed Shane.

"Yeah, but he wasn't that scary once we spoke to him," I said. "But almost by accident, he mentioned that there were a bunch of other bodies buried up here. You could tell that we weren't supposed to know about it though."

"And I don't think we should tell anyone that we do know about it either," I said. "There's something important that went on here, and I want us to be the ones that figure it out."

"I guess so," said Lauren. "But we'll have to tell people eventually, won't we?"

"Sure, but let's take a week or so to work on it," I said. "If the government finds out about this place, there will be hundreds of people crawling all through these woods. There goes Devin and Shane's hiding place and our mystery!"

We all agreed and swore an oath of secrecy. It was getting late in the day, and the last place any of us wanted to be was in these woods with a pile of dead bodies just below us that were covered in neon green fuzz, especially as darkness was approaching.

The four of us grabbed the sides of the trapdoor and strained to lift it closed. We didn't want anyone to stumble across our discovery, so we covered it with several shovelfuls of dirt and then a bunch of the bricks we had unearthed.

We also didn't want anything in the hole to get out.

Chapter 15
THE GRAVES

That night was a long one. I understood what my brothers were feeling when they decided to double up and take a smaller room in the center of the house.

I tried to sleep, but I was constantly hearing noises from the outside. Every time I heard them, I felt compelled to go to my window, fully expecting to see the face of one of the skeletons staring back at me. And when I didn't hear noises, things seemed too quiet. I just knew the dead bodies had escaped and were in my backyard, just below my window, waiting for me to come out.

Lying in bed, I imagined the dead below my window, underneath the creepy willow tree, gathered around the graves. They used their boney, deformed hands to claw at the dirt, trying to free their brethren from beneath the tombstones. I realized that I was being ridiculous, but seeing a cavern full of skeletons in my backyard really had freaked me out.

Then a thought crossed my mind: the two gravesites had been connected somehow. If the other bodies were the same ones listed in the book at the library, it would have been too much of a coincidence for their deaths not to have been related. After all, they all died only about a week apart.

I tossed and turned and stared at the ceiling. It was already past midnight, but sleep was not an option. A continuous stream of questions kept running through my mind.

Why would they be buried in that hole? Were there so many that proper funerals would have been too expensive? How could their deaths have been connected if the others had gotten their flu shots? And why were there so many?

Then it struck me: Maybe it wasn't the flu…maybe it was the flu shots!

I decided that sleep could wait, especially since I was wide awake anyway. I went to my desk and turned on my computer. In a matter of minutes, I was online and running a search using the key words "flu vaccination risks".

Countless articles turned up. Nearly all of them, however, mentioned a disease called Guillain-Barré syndrome or GBS. I clicked on the first one and started reading.

Guillain-Barré Syndrome

Guillain-Barré syndrome (GBS) is a disease of the central nervous system, causing muscle weakness and possible paralysis. Between five and ten percent of patients who develop GBS die from it.

GBS starts as an infection in the lungs. In 1976, the swine flu vaccine was determined to be the leading cause of GBS. The first flu vaccines in the early 1900s caused a much rarer and deadlier form of the disease called violent Guillain-Barré syndrome (VGBS).

Isolated outbreaks of VGBS occurred in the early 1900s and were typified by dementia, excessive appetite, and violent behavior. The disease is considered to be eradicated, as no cases have been reported since the destruction of the early flu vaccine.

Although there are several risks to receiving flu shots, the elderly face a far greater risk of dying from the flu itself. For this reason, it has always been strongly recommended that the elderly or the ill receive yearly vaccinations.

The information seemed to make sense with what we had found. The massive grave could have been dug so that this strange disease could have been contained in this one small area. They were probably buried in the middle of the woods with no grave markers to keep them hidden.

What I couldn't figure out was why the bodies weren't covered in dirt like any other grave. We would have never discovered them if there hadn't been a huge burial room with a wooden ceiling, ten-foot-high walls, and a trapdoor.

There seemed to be something else missing in this puzzle. I couldn't help thinking that I was overlooking something obvious. Something sinister.

I went back to my bed after stealing one more glance at the tombstones. Exhaustion finally forced my brain to stop racing and, in a few minutes, I fell asleep on top of my covers.

Chapter 16
THE GRAVES

I slept in very late the following morning. My body needed to recover from a restless night. Around eleven o'clock, I called Lauren to tell her what I had found out about the flu vaccinations.

Lauren answered the phone with a sleepy, "Hello?"

"Hey, it's Katie. Sounds like you had a sleepless night too."

"Yeah, you're not kidding," she answered. I must have woken up five different times in the middle of the night with different nightmares. Man, your house is freaky!"

"Tell me about it," I said.

"And then I was woken up at six in the morning because my grandma was sick," said Lauren.

"Why did *you* have to get up? What, are you a doctor or something?" I asked sarcastically.

"No, no, my dad was taking care of her, but she was making all kinds of noise. She was screaming and yelling. It's like she's gone crazy or something."

"I'm sorry to hear that," I said. "It sounds horrible."

"My dad gave her a sleeping pill to calm her down," said Lauren. "She was screaming that the light hurt her eyes, and she couldn't stop scratching her skin. She's in her room now with all of the lights out and the blinds drawn. My dad even put up blankets over the windows to make it as dark as possible. He called the doctor, and he's got an appointment for her at two o'clock this afternoon."

"Well, I hope she feels better. It sounds pretty serious."

"Yeah, thanks. But I'm sure she'll be fine. She's pretty tough for an old lady," said Lauren.

"So anyway, last night I was doing some research, and I found some pretty interesting stuff online," I said. "Why don't I come over to see where you live, and we'll work on our mystery?"

"You better not with my grandma sick and all. Why don't I come to your house? We could go back to the clearing again too!"

"I guess so," I said with a little hesitation. "I mean, definitely come on over. It's just...well, I'm not sure if I feel like going back there again after the night I had."

"Aw, come on, you chicken," said Lauren. "I'll see you in a half an hour."

■■■

Lauren's grandmother lay in her bed. The lights were turned off, the shades were pulled down, blankets were hung, and the curtains were closed. The room was as dark as possible for the middle of the afternoon. But the light still irritated her.

She pulled the blankets over her head so that she was completely covered. The sleeping pills were wearing off, and she was becoming more aware of her hunger.

But the hunger wasn't strong enough to make her move into the light. The rashes on her frail skin burned and itched more if they were exposed to daylight.

Her eyes were almost completely shut now, as they had crusted over with the yellowish green puss from the infection oozing out of them.

Her mind no longer knew who or where she was. It knew only two things: stay in the dark and find food, in that order.

But the order was about to change. The desire for nourishment was becoming overwhelming. Soon, hunger pains would outweigh the skin pain.

A few minutes later, she tore the covers off of her and stumbled across the room. Through her partially opened eyes, she could barely make out the light coming in from the outside. She burst through the window, tearing the curtains and shattering the glass, and fell in a clump three feet down to the ground.

Like an animal, she scrambled to her feet and limped as fast as possible into the woods, clawing at her skin, searching desperately for darkness and food.

She blindly hobbled farther back under the canopy of trees, following the smell of fresh meat. Eyes now completely covered in the infection, she stumbled over roots and crawled over the terrain, relying completely on scent for her meal. The yellowish green bile now hung in thick streams from the corners of her mouth, and snarling and gurgling sounds emanated from her throat. The scent led her to a hole under a rotting tree.

Frantically, she dug with her fingernails, searching for the rabbit that had just scurried down into its burrow. The rabbit tried to dig deeper, but it couldn't dig as fast as its predator.

A few minutes later, Lauren's grandmother had her meal. The rabbit was gone in a matter of seconds, leaving her nightgown stained with the drool of infection, dirt from the forest floor, and blood from her dinner. The darkness is what she needed now. She dug deeper with her bloodied fingernails under the base of the tree, and squeezed her emaciated body into the rabbit's former home. There she lay in the moist darkness of the cool earth, waiting for night.

Or for another meal to wander by.

Chapter 17
THE GRAVES

Shortly after our conversation, Lauren arrived at my front door. I was just finishing the last bite of a turkey sandwich.

"Hey," I said after a final swallow. "That was fast."

"I rode my bike," she said. "I figured maybe you'd want to go for a ride, and I could show you around."

"Yeah, we could do that," I said. "But first, let me show you what I found last night."

We went up to my room and sat down at the computer. After a minute or two, we were online and looking at the article on Guillain-Barré syndrome.

I showed her the connection between GBS and flu vaccines. Then I scrolled down to the bottom of the article to the section that discussed VGBS.

"Here, look at this," I said. "This is the part that I wanted you to see."

I read out loud the single paragraph that dealt with the disease and its symptoms.

"See, remember the other day when you said you would never get a flu shot and I said it must have worked because they didn't die from the flu? Well, back then, the vaccine was brand-new. It may have worked for the flu, but what if it caused something far worse?"

"You mean this violent...G-B-whatever thing?" asked Lauren.

"Exactly," I said. "It happened during the same time frame, according to this article, and it could explain why all the Carsons died immediately after getting their flu shots. It might also be why the grave is a giant hole in the ground with no markings."

"I don't get it," said Lauren. "Why wouldn't they be buried like everyone else?"

"Because if these were the only cases of an incurable disease and there was this big quarantine thing, then maybe they didn't want anyone to find it."

"Maybe the government didn't want them found because they knew that they had caused it," said Lauren. "Remember, the article in the library said that after the first two deaths, everyone in the area was forced to get the flu shot. They forced it on them.

Maybe that's why they listed the cause of death in the book as 'unknown'."

∎∎

Devin and Shane felt much braver a day removed from the gruesome discovery. It was also still daylight. They wanted to work on the hideout to make it more of a clubhouse.

But they weren't brave enough to go into the woods without some protection. Devin had a small hatchet that he knew he wasn't supposed to remove from the garage. Shane had a slingshot with real metal ball bearings that his grandfather had given him.

They both knew that the protection that these weapons offered was for peace of mind only. Certainly a roving gang of rotting skeletons would not be deterred by a hatchet and a slingshot.

Once they reached the clearing, they set their weapons down and began their home decorating project. Any large rock was perfect for a campfire ring. The searched the woods for good hideout furniture like a log to sit on and a good stick for roasting marshmallows.

They were careful not to split up.

"Hey, Shane," said Devin. "This log would be a perfect bench. Help me lift it."

"That's great," said Devin. "Let's find three or four just like it and we can put 'em around the campfire."

Devin grabbed one end, and Shane picked up the other. As they raised the log up, something moved in the dirt just behind it, and it startled both of them. They dropped the log and jumped backwards a few steps. Just behind the log was a large hole in the ground.

"What was that?" whispered Shane.

"I don't know," said Devin in a low voice. "It looks like some sort of an animal den, like a fox or something."

Both boys quietly took a few steps closer. Devin picked up a stick and slowly poked it into the dark hole.

With a jolt, Grandma's bloody hand reached out, grabbed the stick, and pulled hard. Devin instinctively let go of the stick and fell backwards into Shane. They scrambled to their feet and moved away, not taking their eyes off of whatever was buried in the hole.

Grandma was not happy with being poked by something that was not edible, and she started clawing her way out. She couldn't see, but she could definitely smell flesh nearby.

Devin and Shane saw the ground start to churn violently, and they stood and stared at it, frozen with fear.

Grandma had pulled herself halfway out of the hole. She was completely covered in dirt, and her skin was falling off in places. Her back was hunched in a horribly contorted fashion, and she was incapable of standing completely erect.

The boys screamed and turned to run, but Shane tripped over a fallen branch. Grandma squeezed the rest of her body out of the hole and started crawling after him like a giant, nasty insect.

Shane shrieked in terror but didn't move. He was on his back with his legs kicking frantically in the air as he watched the figure advance on him, mouth agape and dripping discolored liquid. Devin grabbed him under his arms and yanked him to his feet just as Grandma lunged for his legs. They leaped over the branch as Grandma caught hold of Shane's shoe and pulled it off of his foot. The boys ran full speed, darting through the foliage with Grandma trying to pursue, but because of her blindness, she stumbled over the ground and crashed into branches.

Devin and Shane shot out of the woods and turned to look back behind them. Grandma reached the edge of the tree line, but the light on her skin was too painful and she still had a stomach full of a recent meal. She stopped the chase and returned to her home in the earth among the cool, moist soil under the tree.

She would hunt again in the darkness.

Chapter 18
THE GRAVES

Devin and Shane burst through the front door, screaming like they had just been attacked by a crazy old lady who was trying to eat them.

"MOM! DAD! HELP!"

They ran in circles, yelling hysterically, until my mom came running in from the kitchen. Five seconds later, Lauren and I were down the steps, and my father ran in from the garage. The boys could barely breathe, and they were covered with sweat.

"What's wrong? What happened?" my mom shrieked.

Devin immediately began yelling, "We were in the woods, and this monster came crawling..."

Shane yelled right over top of him, "This thing attacked us from under the ground!"

Both continued at this pace so that neither of them could be understood.

"Slow down!" my father interrupted. "Now, wait a second. Okay, now one at a time. Devin, you first."

Devin took a deep breath.

"We were out in the woods playing around, and this monster came out of this hole in the ground."

Shane couldn't hold it in any longer: "And it came after us and took my shoe! It was trying to eat me!"

"What are you talking about?" my dad said, not believing a single word except for the part where they were in the woods. "There's no such thing as monsters. You know that. It must have been some sort of animal you saw."

"No way, Dad!" said Devin. "This thing was in a hole, but it was wearing clothes! It was some sort of human!"

"And it took the shoe right off of my foot!" Shane screamed once again.

"All right, maybe you're right," my father said. "It's getting dark soon. Tomorrow, we'll go back there together, and you can show me where this werewolf or whatever lives."

"I don't like this, Rob," said my mother. "What if it's a hermit or some sort of insane person or something that lives in the woods? Maybe we should call the police."

"What am I going to tell them? There's a monster in the woods? Can you please come and get it?" my dad joked. "Let's just wait until morning so I can investigate a little myself first. We don't want to be seen as the new crazy neighbors."

"Well, okay, I guess," said my mom. "But you all are in for the night. And no more going into the woods until your father takes a look around."

"No problem!" Shane readily agreed. "I'm never leaving this house again anyhow!"

Even though it wasn't the best timing, I asked my mom if Lauren could spend the night. After a few minutes of begging, pleading, and promising we'd go to bed at a reasonable hour, she finally agreed.

"But let me call Lauren's father to see if it's all right," said my mom.

She picked up the phone. Lauren's father picked up the phone on the first ring. My mom seemed startled by the tone of his voice. "Uh, hello...this is Jennifer Pribble, Katie's mom?"

All I could hear was her side of the conversation

"She sure is. As a matter of fact, the girls are begging for a sleepover, and I told them that I would give you a call to see if was okay...Oh, well, we can do it some other time that's more convenient for you all...Oh my goodness. Well, can we help? Would you like us to bring Lauren home?...Absolutely, please let me know what else we can do. How about if my husband comes over to help you look for her?...Well, we'll take good care of her, and I'll call you in the morning to see how things are. She is welcome to stay here as long as you need. I hope everything works out okay."

When she hung up the phone, my mother turned to us and said, "Okay, girls, it's fine, but remember, I don't want you up all night. And don't be scaring your brothers with a bunch of ghost stories. I want this to be a peaceful evening."

Chapter 19
THE GRAVES

Lauren and I spent most of the night watching television, playing board games, and just hanging out in my room. My brothers spent most of the evening looking out of all the windows in the house for the monster that had attacked them.

They stayed upstairs and peered through their windows, watching the edge of the woods. It was twilight, and the boys were convinced that the monster would come back for them under the cover of night.

Within the hour, dusk had fully given way to darkness. It was only a matter of minutes until their predictions would prove to be correct.

Lauren and I were busy decorating my room by taping pictures of magazines onto the walls. As I climbed onto my desk with some tape and a picture of Marilyn Monroe, some movement caught my eye in the backyard.

I put my head closer to the glass and peered out of the window.

"Lauren, look at this quick!"

From out of the edge of the woods, the creature that the boys had described was walking towards the house. It lumbered slowly and deliberately with its hands outstretched, blindly feeling its way through the darkness.

Moments later, we realized that the boys had seen it too. They came running out of their room, screaming in terror, "Mom, Dad...IT'S HERE! LOCK THE DOORS!"

Within seconds, they were down the stairs, each yelling louder than the other. Lauren and I were two steps behind, screaming along with them.

From our rantings, my father was able to figure that some sort of creature was out back, but that was about it.

"Okay, hold on a second," he said, trying to calm us down. "Now, Katie, you saw this thing too?"

I was so scared that my eyes were tearing up as I spoke and my voice was quivering. "Yes, I saw it walking across the backyard towards the house. It's right outside," I said, pointing to the back window.

"What was it?" my dad asked. "Was it a person or maybe an animal?"

"It looked like a person...I guess...like an old witch," I stammered. "It kind of looked like ...like a zombie or something."

My dad turned to Lauren, "And did you see this too?"

Lauren merely nodded her head and mumbled, "Uh-huh."

"All right, you guys stay here," said my dad. I'll go outside and take a look around."

He went to the garage and returned a few seconds later with a baseball bat in his right hand and a flashlight in his left.

Without hesitation, he walked out of the front door, and we were left in the living room waiting for him to return...hopefully.

Chapter 20
THE GRAVES

Devin and Shane were too scared to speak. Their
encounter with the monster earlier in the day had been
terrifying, but seeing her again put them in a state of
shock. Lauren and I, although clearly frightened, were
also curious.

The bottom floor of our house had many
windows. In fact, from where we stood in the living
room, we could see the outside from any direction. We
had turned the outside lights on, but that only
illuminated the front porch and the back corner of the
house.

My mother, Lauren, and I each stood in a different window, trying to catch a glimpse of any movement. The boys sat together on the couch, as far away as possible from any window.

Out in the back, near the tree line, I could see the beam of my father's flashlight sweeping back and forth across the woods. I peered more closely, with my hands touching the glass and my face between them, but the glare from the inside lights made it difficult to see.

"Hey, guys, turn off the lights in here," I said to Devin and Shane. "We can see better with them off."

"No way!" said Shane. "Are you crazy?"

"No, seriously," I said. "We'll be able to see better. And more importantly, the thing won't be able to see us."

In a flash, the boys had turned off both lamps next to the couch that they were sitting on.

I could see better almost immediately, but it really made the night much eerier. In the dark, the silence of the room became more noticeable.

I could see the silhouette of my father carrying the flashlight, making his way back to the house, sweeping the beam across the yard. Suddenly, he stopped about thirty feet away and shined his light at the corner of the house where we were standing. I could hear him yell something but couldn't quite make it out. He started running in our direction.

Out of the darkness, a hand smashed through the window that Lauren and I were looking through.

Her grandma's gnarled and bloody hand, with a huge chunk of glass protruding from the knuckle, grabbed hold of Lauren's shirt as she tried to jump back. Lauren screamed and pulled away as hard as she could as more glass shattered into the darkened room.

The deranged grandma smashed her other hand through the window and pulled herself through the shards of broken glass.

Slowly and deliberately, she rose from her knees, totally blind from her eyes being crusted over. She was covered in blood and dirt from burying herself in the woods, and fresh wounds had just opened up from breaking through the window. Her skin was so damaged that, in some places, the bones were actually visible. Animalistic sounds came out of her mouth from deep inside her gut. She advanced on us, snarling and growling.

Screaming, we backed out of the living room and into the hallway where the light was on. The monster lumbered forward and let out a howl of pain when the light touched her skin.

Once the creature was out of the darkness, Lauren thought she recognized her grandmother by her torn nightclothes.

"Grandma? Grandma? Is that you?" pleaded Lauren, sobbing as she kept backing up. "Everything's going to be okay. It's me, Lauren."

For a moment, her grandma paused, possibly out of some sort of recognition. The sound of her granddaughter's voice triggered a brief second of memory.

At that moment, my father threw open the front door and shined the flashlight directly into Grandma's face.

"Everybody back away!" he commanded.

Then, with amazing quickness, the monster lurched forward, grabbed Lauren by the neck, and opened her jaws to bite into her meal.

My father charged at her just before her remaining good teeth could puncture the skin of Lauren's neck. He shoved the creature as hard as he could, sending her tumbling down the basement steps. She landed with a sickening thud and the sound of a bone breaking like a tree branch. She lay there on her back, with her arm clearly in the direction that it was not meant to be bent, motionless. We stared at the sprawled body at the bottom of the stairs in complete silence. Only Lauren's muffled cried and heavy breathing were audible.

Then, with a primal roar, she sat up and began crawling up the steps after us like an insect. My dad slammed the door just before she reached the top step and slid the deadbolt lock shut.

Grandma growled as she clawed at the door. We heard her ram her body against it. With every thrust into the door, the monster that had been Lauren's grandma screamed in pain.

The hinges groaned, and the wood buckled, but she couldn't break through.

The trap seemed to be holding....for now.

Chapter 21
THE GRAVES

"Jen, call the police!" my dad shouted to my mother.

We stood about ten feet away, staring at the door, hoping it would hold. After what seemed like an eternity, the pounding and scratching finally stopped.

My father approached it carefully, trying not to agitate the monster any further. He quietly placed his ear on the door to listen for any movement.

Slowly, the old decrepit hands inched out from underneath the door. I screamed in horror for my dad to move, and he jumped away, leaving the gruesome fingers searching for something to grab.

A moment later, the bloody fingers stopped moving, and the only sound that could be heard was our own rapid breathing. My dad was the only one with enough nerve to speak.

"Lauren, is that really your grandmother?" he asked.

"I...I....I think so," she answered with confusion on her face and tears in her eyes. "It kind of looked like her. But what was wrong with her?"

"Honey, there's something you need to know," said my mother. "When I called your father earlier, he said your grandmother was very sick and had escaped from the house. The police have been looking for her, but he didn't want you to be worried about it."

Lauren looked very bewildered. "It's like she was trying to kill us. Why is she acting that way?"

"I don't know. I'm sure she doesn't even know where she is right now," said my mother. "Let me call your father so he can come over, and maybe he'll be able to calm her down."

We all sat there not being sure what to feel. We were all scared of the thing trapped on the other side of the door, but knowing it was Lauren's grandmother, we were also concerned for Lauren.

After about five minutes, the police knocked on the door. My father opened it quickly, and I could see the police car lights illuminating our entire front yard with splashes of red and blue.

A second car sped up the driveway and came to a screeching stop. Mr. Sheridan, Lauren's father, jumped out and ran over, leaving the door open behind him.

"Where is she?" he said breathlessly. "Lauren, are you all right?"

Lauren bit her lip and touched the bite on her neck. "Yeah, I'm okay, I guess."

"Come on in, Bill," said my father. "Officer, this is Bill Sheridan. His mother is the one who we think is trapped inside our basement."

"Yes, we meet Mr. Sheridan earlier. We've been looking for Mrs. Sheridan all day," said the officer. "But I'm confused. Didn't you say on the call that you had some sort of *creature* locked in your basement?"

"Right behind that door," answered my dad. "But I gotta tell ya, this isn't your ordinary grandmother."

My father went on to tell them about the boys in the woods and the attack on the house through the window.

After hearing the story, the police, deciding that they would not need their guns to capture an elderly grandma, walked over to the locked door.

"Mrs. Sheridan?" the officer yelled. "This is the police. We're here to help you. We're going to open the door. I want you to stay calm. We are not going to hurt you."

Then the second policeman reached up and slid the bolt open.

Chapter 22
THE GRAVES

Lauren and I backed away to the end of the hallway. Devin and Shane sprinted out of sight and cowered under the dining room table.

One of the officers had his hand on the doorknob, and the other stood by, ready to subdue what he thought was a frail, elderly woman.

In silence, the officer mouthed a count of, "One...two...three," and quickly jerked the door open.

There was nothing there. The carpet was stained with blood and dirt, but the stairway to the basement was empty.

"Sir, was this door always like this?" the policeman pointed to the inside of the door, which was entirely shredded into splinters. Red stains of blood dripped down the ruts that had been scraped into the wood.

Lauren and I glanced at each other, remembering what the underside of the trapdoor had looked like in the woods.

"My gosh, no, sir," said my father. "This is a brand-new house."

The officers looked at each other with raised eyebrows. They were obviously surprised by how much damage had been done. It looked like a wolf had been trapped on the other side, not a sick, elderly grandmother.

"Sir, we'll need you to stay up here with your family."

"Oh, don't worry, that's not a problem," my dad said with relief.

One of the policemen pulled out his baton and his flashlight and proceeded slowly down the stairs. The other took his gun out of his holster and followed closely behind.

The next few minutes seemed to last forever. My father and Mr. Sheridan waited at the top of the stairs while the rest of us stayed a safe distance away in the dining room.

Eventually, one of the policemen called up to my dad, "Sir, could you come down here for a second?"

My father and Mr. Sheridan walked down cautiously into the basement, unsure of what they were about to see. I tiptoed a few steps behind them, wanting to see firsthand what was going on.

At the far end of the basement, behind the tons of unpacked moving boxes, a small window had been smashed. With barely enough room to squeeze through, the creature had escaped from its trap. Torn pieces of her bloody nightgown remained on the jagged shards of glass in the window.

The creature was on the loose again.

The police stayed a bit longer to finish their paperwork, but then they were gone. They assured us that they were on patrol and that they would keep checking on our house throughout the night.

My parents began discussing where we would stay. I t was nearly midnight at this point, and the nearest decent hotel was at least a half hour away. But the monster had already broken two windows in our house and could easily return to the same place.

They decided that it would be okay to remain in the house if we all stayed together, including Lauren and her father. The thought was that there would be safety in numbers. Mr. Sheridan and my father would stand guard on the bottom floor while the rest of us would stay in our rooms with the doors locked.

Devin and Shane slept with my mother in her bed, and Lauren and I stayed in my room...with the lights on. Daylight could not come soon enough.

Chapter 23
THE GRAVES

I was scared out of my mind! Lauren and I stayed in my room, but knowing that the creature was out there was completely unnerving.

Discovering that it was Lauren's grandmother was even more disturbing.

I kept picturing her blindly wandering out of the woods toward our house. And the boys' tale of her buried in the dirt, waiting to attack them, was simply horrifying. But I didn't want to talk about it with Lauren because, after all, it was her grandmother.

And then a thought came to my mind. Lauren's grandmother wasn't the only thing scary in the woods. I finally made the connection.

"Lauren, I've got it!" I said. "I've figured it out!"

"Figured what out?" she asked.

"Your grandmother! She must have gotten VGBS!"

"How could that be?" she asked. "Remember, the article said it hasn't been around for a hundred years or something."

"Yeah, I know," I said. "But think about it. All of those bodies were buried with that disease. That's probably why they were hidden in the first place...to bury the disease! Don't you remember the cloud of green stuff that came out when we opened it up?"

"You mean we let it out?" Lauren asked, horrified.

"I think so," I said. "Just look at your grandma's symptoms. She's acting crazy, and she definitely has the violent behavior. And remember, it all started with the skin rash."

"But that stuff could have spread anywhere," Lauren protested. "Why would my grandma be the only one to get it? And why don't we have it?"

"Maybe she's not the only one who has it," I said. "Maybe there are others."

Chapter 24
THE GRAVES

"You're right," said Lauren. "If my grandma got it and we live a mile away, then who knows how many other people might get it?"

"Or already have it," I said. "Either way, we have to tell our parents what we know."

"You're right," said Lauren. "We could be responsible for the next Black Plague or something."

It took a few minutes, but I managed to get enough nerve to walk back downstairs. It felt so much safer up in my room, away from all of the windows on the bottom floor.

My dad and Mr. Sheridan were sitting on the couch watching television. The baseball bat lay on the coffee table in front of them.

"Hey, Dad," I started. "Did Lauren's grandma stop by for another visit?" I said with a feeble attempt at humor to hide the fact that we had caused this problem.

"Well, not yet," he answered. "What are you guys doing down here? It's one o'clock in the morning. You need to stay upstairs and at least try to get some sleep."

"There is something we need to talk to you about," I said, swallowing hard. "We know why Lauren's grandmother is acting this way. And it's kind of our fault."

"Look, I know this has been difficult," Mr. Sheridan said. "But you have to understand, sometimes, when people get older, they get sick. It's very common for someone as old as Lauren's grandmother to have their minds affected by illness."

"Oh, I know, Dad," said Lauren. "But look at this."

She handed him the article from the Internet on VGBS.

"We think we have uncovered a secret that wasn't supposed to ever be found," I said.

I started from the beginning, when I wanted to learn about the tombstones and how Old Man Miller had told us of the other bodies. I told them about the

quarantine and the connection to the flu virus and
VGBS.

"Katie, this is very interesting research," my dad
said. "But I don't think Mrs. Sheridan would have
caught a virus that's been dormant for over a hundred
years. Anyway, why would any of this be your fault?"

"Wait, we're not quite finished," I said. "Two
days ago, we were back in the woods, and we found the
hidden graves."

"What do you mean 'hidden'?" asked my father.

"Well, it wasn't exactly a grave...Buried in the
ground, underneath a layer of bricks, we found a giant
room with a locked trapdoor. When we opened it, this
horrible-smelling, green cloud of dust poured out into
the air. The trapdoor covered a huge grave with about
fifteen bodies lying in it. I think that when we opened
the door, we released the disease."

"You found a bunch of dead bodies buried in our
backyard and didn't tell us about it?" asked my dad.

"Well...pretty much," I said sheepishly. "I figured
that if I told you, then you would call the police. If the
word had gotten out, then we wouldn't have gotten to
solve the mystery. Pretty lame, I know."

"Well, I'm glad you came to me now. You've
certainly done your research, and it sounds like you
might be on to something. Tomorrow, in the daylight, I
want you to take Mr. Sheridan and me to see the grave."

"But what about the disease?" I asked. "How do
we know if Lauren's grandmother isn't the only one?"

"That's a good point," said Mr. Sheridan. "There aren't a lot of people around here, but the few that are, are very elderly. Maybe we'll visit a few tomorrow and check on some of them."

Lauren and I retreated back up to the safety of my room, where we were finally able to settle down a bit. I felt a little relieved that somebody else now knew about what was possibly becoming a heath disaster.

Somehow, by sharing the information with my dad, I felt that things would be okay, that maybe the whole county wasn't going to turn into evil zombies.

Chapter 25
THE GRAVES

I awoke the next morning to the smell of bacon and eggs for breakfast. Once we were downstairs, I saw that my father had covered the broken window with a plastic trash bag to keep the bugs out and the air conditioning in.

"Good morning, y'all," said my dad. "Did you have pleasant dreams?" he said sarcastically.

"Yeah, right," I mumbled.

"We went searching in the woods this morning, and we found the graves you were talking about," said my dad.

"You found it? Did you look inside?" I asked.

"Yep, we got it open. That is an amazing discovery you came across. You know, the more I thought about it, the more sense your ideas made. So after breakfast, I'm going to visit a few of the neighbors."

"By the way, Lauren," said my mother as she put a plate of eggs on the table, "your father went home to check on things there. He said he would pick you up a little later."

"Dad, can we go with you?" I asked.

"Nah, I think you'd better stay here. After all, what if you are right?" he asked. "It might not be safe."

"Hey, no fair," I said. "This is our mystery. Plus, we'd be safer with you than by ourselves."

"Well, I guess so," said my dad. "It probably wouldn't hurt to have a few more eyes with me."

A short while later, the three of us drove in my father's pickup truck down Cypress Creek Road towards town.

"There's not a ton of houses around here, maybe seven or eight, and I'm sure that elderly people live in every one from the looks of them," said my father.

In a minute or two, we came to an old, rusty mailbox along the side of the road. The driveway was long and twisted, and the old oak trees that lined the path made it so that we couldn't see the house from the road.

Unfortunately, my dad decided that this should be the first stop. He pulled onto the dirt path and proceeded slowly over the bumpy terrain.

The place was a mess. Old rusted cars and other pieces of junk were scattered about. We passed an old wooden shed with half of the roof caved in. A scraggly old dog lay on the side of the dirt road, staring at us menacingly. It howled a deep bark or two and managed to climb to its feet, but did not have enough energy to take any steps to follow after us.

Up ahead, we could see what probably used to be a cute farmhouse. But now, the shutters were crooked, and there was no way to tell what color the paint used to be. It was just dreary, weathered wood at this point.

"Talk about your fixer-upper," said my father.

"Yeah, why don't we skip this house?" I said, hoping all of the neighbors didn't live like this.

"Oh, don't worry, I'm sure these people are just too old to take proper care of this place. I think we just found a great summer project for you two," he said, laughing.

"You're crazy if you think I'm coming back here!" I said.

My dad got out of the truck, and Lauren and I followed. From where we stood, I could see that the front door stood completely open. We walked up the porch steps and realized immediately that something was wrong.

The screen door lay on the ground, and it had a huge gash down the center. My father stepped over it and knocked on the wide-open door.

"Hello? Is anyone home?" he called.

Lauren and I stepped forward to get a peek inside. The place was trashed. Curtains had been ripped down, and a coffee table had been smashed and turned over in the middle of the floor. The television was lying sideways on the floor and was still turned on.

"Well, it looks like they may have had the same houseguest that we did," said my father.

"Or maybe they've got the same virus that our houseguest has," I said.

And then I realized that we were being watched.

Chapter 26
THE GRAVES

From up on the steps, I saw something move.

"Hello? Anybody home?" my father called out.

It was dark at the top of the stairway. Dad went a few steps up and called again, "Is everybody okay?"

And then, like a flash, a scrawny brown cat tore down the steps past Lauren and me and took off outside.

Dad continued upstairs to take a quick look around. The stairs creaked loudly with every step. Lauren and I stayed close to the doorway in case we needed to make a quick exit. It was freaky being in a stranger's house, especially this one.

"Well, something is going on here," said my father as he came down the stairway. "But this place is empty. I saw another house just past this one down the road. Let's go check it out."

The driveway to the next home was short, and we could see part of the house from the main road. Everything seemed much neater and cleaner. There was no junk lying around, and there was actually grass growing in the front yard.

But we could see immediately that something was wrong here too.

On the second floor, the side window was smashed out, and pieces of glass covered the ground underneath it. Splintered pieces of the wooden window frame were also lying about. I got out of the truck and walked over to the debris.

I reached down and picked up a bent pair of eyeglasses. One of the lenses was covered with blood. I looked up at the window. Pieces of the wood frame had been snapped in half and protruded outward.

"It looks like somebody fell out of that window," my father said.

"Or jumped," said Lauren.

"Or was pushed," I said.

"Either way, that's a heck of a fall," said my dad.

"Well, where are they now?" I asked.

"Let's go home and call the police," said my father. "Your mother and the boys are there alone."

We hopped back into the truck and headed up Cypress Creek Road towards our house.

"You know, this place is even deader than usual," said Lauren. "I mean, we haven't seen another person or even a car all morning."

A moment later, our driveway was in sight. But instead of making a left, my father pulled over to the right side of the road in front of Old Man Miller's place. There was no driveway because the thicket had grown so densely over the years that it basically ceased to exist.

"Let me make one more stop here and check on Mr. Miller," said my dad. "It'll just take a second."

Lauren and I glanced at each other and cautiously got out of the truck. While my father went up the front steps, she and I stood among the weeds, waiting.

My father pulled open the screen door. The creaking was so loud that knocking didn't seem necessary, but he did it anyway.

Almost immediately, Old Man Miller was at the door, but this time he wasn't opening it.

"WHO IS IT?" he growled from behind the closed door.

"It's Rob Pribble, your neighbor from across the street."

After a pause, the series of sliding bolts and turning locks and chains being removed began.

Eventually, he cracked the door open, but only a couple of inches.

"I'm kinda busy right now," he grumbled. His hand on the door was dark brown with dirt. "What do you want?"

"Uh, well, there have been a few problems with some of the residents in the area, and I thought I'd come by to check on you. We haven't met. I'm Rob."

My father reached out to shake hands, but Old Man Miller didn't budge.

"Well, I'm fine. Nice to meet you," said Mr. Miller.

And with that, he slammed the door shut. My dad turned and gave us a comical look of surprise.

"You know," said my dad as we walked back to the truck, "he might be acting crazy too, but something tells me that's the way he always is."

Chapter 27
THE GRAVES

As we pulled up into our driveway, my mother saw us coming and met us at the front porch. When she saw the look on my father's face, she instantly asked, "What's wrong? What did you find?"

My father began describing the two houses we visited. He told her something was definitely going on, but just wasn't sure what.

As my mother listened intently, something distracted her in the distance. I turned to see what had caught her attention.

Walking briskly up the driveway and looking very irritated was Old Man Miller. Seeing him off of his property with his long, crazy hair under his cowboy hat, his crooked, yellow teeth, and his wild, darting eyes was like seeing a ghost.

The same person who had just slammed the door in my father's face was now moving with shocking speed right to our front door!

"Hey, Mr. Miller," my dad said from a distance. "Everything okay?"

He didn't respond until he was standing directly in front of my father. He got uncomfortably close to him.

"We need to talk," he said in a low voice, while his eyes darted all around like he was afraid he was being watched or something. "Inside."

He glanced at me as he turned and didn't say a word. I was sure that he was mad at Lauren and me for bothering him at his house. I didn't know what he was going to do, and it made me nervous.

We all did exactly what we were told and followed my father and Old Man Miller into our house.

Mr. Miller started, "First off, what sort of problems was you talkin' 'bout before?"

"Well, maybe you saw last night that the police were over here," said my dad.

"I don't see nothin' at night," said Old Man Miller. "'Round these parts, that's the safest way."

I didn't know what to make of that ominous statement.

"Okay then, I think you know my daughter, Katie, and her friend Lauren. Lauren's grandmother, as it turns out, is very ill and has been missing for a few days now. Last night she smashed through one of our windows in the back and was just going crazy.

"To make a long story short, the police came, but she escaped before they could catch her. Anyway, the girls have been doing a little research, and they think maybe she's caught a virus that was around in the area near the turn of the century.

"I came by your house because I was checking on some elderly neighbors. I was down at the Dills' and the Youngs', but there's nobody there. By the looks of things, they have been attacked also."

Old Man Miller looked shocked and terrified. He turned to Lauren and me and asked, "Have you girls been snoopin' 'round for dem graves?"

"Yes, sir," I answered meekly. "And we found them in the woods."

"What do you mean you *found* dem?" asked Old Man Miller. "Did you find the door?"

I just nodded my head.

"Did you open it?"

I nodded again.

"Aw, cripes...things are about to get real bad 'round here!"

Chapter 28
THE GRAVES

"What do you mean by *bad*, exactly?" asked my mother. "Do you know what all of this is about?"

"Yep, sure do. And it all has to do with them there graves," said Old Man Miller. "But I got a question for you," he said, turning and looking at Lauren. "How old is yer grandma?"

"I think she's eighty-three," said Lauren.

Old Man Miller looked very concerned. His forehead wrinkled and he asked, "Did she happen to get flu shots?"

"Yes, sir," said Lauren. "Every year."

"Oh, this is bad," he mumbled. He went over and peeked past the curtains through the front window. "Let me ask y'all one more question," he said quietly. "Do you all get flu shots?"

My mother answered this one, "Well, actually no. We've never seemed to really need them."

"How 'bout you," he snapped at Lauren as if she had done something wrong.

"No, my grandma got them because she was old, but my father didn't make me get one," she answered.

"All right then, you all should be okay, but we don't have much time to get ready," said Old Man Miller.

"Shouldn't we call the police or the Department of Health or something?" asked my father.

"No, no, NOOOO," said Old Man Miller, shaking his head vehemently. "That's the *last* thing we need! Let me give you a little history 'bout dat grave in the woods. Back in 1910, I was five years old. That makes me ninety-nine. Back then, a real bad flu came through these parts, and people started dyin'. Well, the gub'ment was just developin' this newfangled flu shot. They swooped in and forced everyone who lived 'round here to get one. Said it was fer our own good."

"See, Dad," I said. "It's just like I told you! The people died from the flu shot!"

"Well, not exactly," said Old Man Miller. "The flu shot didn't kill nobody. But it made 'em monsters. Everyone went crazy cuz they all got that shot.

Everybody cep my mother and me. See, when this all started happenin', I was one off the first ones to get sick. My ma took me to the hospital in Baltimore, and I got a different batch of that vaccine. After I got better and we came home, there was nobody left.

"I spent my whole life tryin' to figger it out, and I always thought it had to be that experimental batch of flu shots they gave everybody. Maybe that's what it was, but anyhow, once that door was opened, the 1910 virus came back. But this time it looks like it got to folks that got regular, good flu shots. And that's a whole mess of people!"

"So why not call the Health Department?" I asked. "I'm sure they must have learned something about it over the past one hundred years."

"You don't understand," said Old Man Miller. "If they find out 'bout this, you ain't never leaving Cypress Creek. This disease makes monsters! I'm talkin' 'bout the walking dead that are craving healthy flesh. Human flesh.

"Last time the army came in and quarantined the place. The whole town was wiped out. They didn't let anyone go cuz they couldn't tell who had it and who could spread it. If you call the authorities, yer diggin' yer own grave right here in Cypress Creek."

Chapter 29
THE GRAVES

As crazy he appeared while he was telling his story, the old man's words sounded convincing. Besides, no one in the room was going to disagree with him anyway.

"Okay, all this seems to make sense," said my father. "But if we don't call the authorities, what can we do? Just lock the doors and hope for the best?"

"Can't do that," said Old Man Miller. "See, you don't understand. These things just keep getting worse. The hungrier they get, the meaner they get. And there ain't no way to stop 'em except to bury 'em. And we're not just talkin' 'bout one anymore. There could be twenty or thirty of 'em."

"So how do we protect ourselves?" asked my dad. "The closest things I have to weapons are kitchen knives and baseball bats."

"Weapons won't work nohow," barked Old Man Miller, shaking his head. "We got to starve 'em. That's what they did back then. You all need to get to a safe place, and I mean right quick. By night, this place will be crawling with monsters."

"Are you saying we should just leave?" asked my mother.

"Nah, if you left, your place would be torn apart. And you wouldn't know if it was safe to come back nohow. And the gub'ment would find you. Come on over to my house. I've been getting my place ready for this for fifty years. Ain't nobody gettin' in there! Plus, we got to stop 'em before they spread."

"So that's why you don't have any windows," I said.

"That's right. There's only one way in and one way out. Now c'mon, get this house locked up and head on over. We don't have a ton of time."

Old Man Miller shuffled back down our driveway, and shortly after, Lauren's father pulled up. The adults went outside to talk about the situation in private, leaving the four kids to ourselves.

Devin spoke first, "I'm not going over to that crazy man's haunted house!"

"Yeah, I know," said Shane. "Can you imagine how creepy looking it must be on the inside?"

"Guys, we might not have much of a choice," I said. "But don't worry, Mom and Dad will think of something."

To my amazement, after a few minutes, my parents returned and told us they had accepted Old Man Miller's invitation. A little while later, we were locking all the doors and walking towards the scariest house I had ever seen.

Chapter 30
THE GRAVES

The walk down our driveway was stressful. I was no longer trying to solve a mystery; I was trying to stay alive. Everyone was completely quiet, as if we were walking to a funeral. In fact, the entire world seemed to be afraid. There were no squirrels moving in the trees or birds flying in the sky.

Every little sound I made seemed to announce my movement, so I tried to walk as softly as possible. Although my parents tried to downplay it, I knew that I was hiding from predators and we were their prey. The monsters could be anywhere.

The overgrowth of branches and vines at Old Man Miller's fortress seemed like the perfect hiding place for the creatures. Each step through the brush was terrifying. But even more frightening were the front steps leading to the unknown of the inside of the house.

I walked up the creaking steps, trying to stay as close to my father as possible. The porch was in such disrepair that it felt like it could collapse at any moment. We waited as my father knocked on the door.

"Who is it?" barked Old Man Miller from behind the closed door.

"It's the Pribbles and Sheridans," my dad yelled back.

After a pause, the unlocking began. A full minute later, the door finally opened.

"All right, hurry up. Get in here," he ordered. But when he saw Lauren's father, he put his hand in the middle of his chest. "Hold on, hold on there," he snapped. "Who are you?"

Mr. Sheridan was a bit startled, but he managed to answer quickly, "I'm Lauren's father, Bill. My mother's the one with the virus."

"Have you had yer flu shot?" he said, almost yelling.

"No, sir, I'm as healthy as an ox," Mr. Sheridan answered.

"All right, fine," said Old Man Miler. "Just checking."

The inside of the house was just as strange as the outside. The area that we walked into was just a long hallway. Instead of having other rooms or stairs branching off to either side, all that was visible were two rows of closed doors.

After we stepped inside, he slammed the heavy front door and relocked everything.

"All right, everybody," he grumbled. "Stay close and follow me. And keep these kids behind you."

We followed, huddled together, down the hallway past all the identical-looking closed doors. Everything was the same color. The walls, ceiling, and floor were all made of dark brown planks of wood. Only a single light bulb, dangling from the ceiling, provided anything out of the ordinary.

Ahead, I saw a hauntingly familiar sight. Positioned sideways across the hallway floor was another huge trapdoor just like the one in the woods.

I looked at Lauren, wondering if the contents would be the same.

"Okay, grab a handle and help me with this," Old Man Miller said to my dad.

They pulled it open to reveal another deep hole in the ground. The light bulb overhead was bright enough that we could see that the hole was empty.

"This is my basement," said Old Man Miller. "And we're gonna need it tonight."

But this wasn't a normal basement. The steps had been removed. The walls were not made of dirt like the grave in the woods. These walls were made of stone. And the most noticeable part of the basement was that it was absolutely empty.

Old Man Miller was to bury the creatures under his house.

Chapter 31
THE GRAVES

"Wh – what kind of basement is that?" I asked.

"It's gonna be a grave," said Old Man Miller. "I built it just like the one they had to use a hundred years ago."

"You mean we're going to have to bury Lauren's gra—I mean that monster in there?" asked my father, glancing nervously at Mr. Sheridan.

"Not just Lauren's grandma, but everybody else 'round these parts," said Old Man Miller. "And we're not doin' the buryin'. They're gonna do that demselves."

"What do you mean by *everyone else*?" asked my mom.

"Well, ma'am, you see, back in 1910, whoever got dem flu shots, they turned into these creatures. But now, it ain't just that one old batch that is the problem. Her grandma weren't even born till ten years after that. It looks to me that the virus that was released will react with *any* flu shot. I don't know if you seen folk 'round these parts, but they're old. The only young people around are you all. And old folk always get their flu shots. Specially in Cypress Creek. Heck, they thought that was the only thing protecting them. Now hurry up, we don't have much time."

"Well, how are we supposed to stop these things?" Mr. Sheridan asked.

"There ain't no stoppin' 'em. I heard stories 'bout 'em. They're already dead. They gotta keep eating flesh. Any kind of meat will do, but human's what they really want. They can't see nuffin, but they can smell you a mile away. And even though they're old, they're strong as bulls because they're so crazy. We can't stop 'em, but we can trap 'em. C'mon, I'll show you."

He opened up one of the many hallway doors, and we followed him into what looked like a fairly normal living room. It was well lit and had real furniture and everything. It obviously used to be a normal home. Once we were all in, Mr. Miller locked a huge sliding bolt behind us. On the same side of the room, just a bit farther down the wall, was another door just like the one we just came through.

After unlocking the bolt on that door, he led us right back into the hallway. Only this time, we were on the other side of the trapdoor.

"We're right back where we started from," said Lauren.

"Except this time you're on the safe side," said Old Man Miller. "See, this will be where *we* stand."

"So wait...we're the bait?" asked my dad. "Are you saying that we're supposed to stand here so those monsters can try to eat us?"

"That's the plan," said Old Man Miller with a completely straight face. "Now hurry up and get ready cuz it's getting late!"

"You know, I really don't think this is going to work for us," said my father. "I think we'll head on over to our car and spend the night out of town somewhere. But thanks anyway. You're welcome to come with us."

"Good idea, honey," said my mother.

"I'm tellin' ya. It's the only way," yelled Old Man Miller as he trailed after us heading back through the living room. "You're gonna get eaten alive out there!"

My dad stopped a few steps from the front entrance of the house. "Mr. Miller, thanks a lot for the advice, but I think we'll have to take our chances."

A minute later, the door had successfully been unlocked, and we stepped out onto the porch.

Then I saw them.

Across the street, heading up the driveway to our house, was an elderly couple. As soon as they heard the screen door close behind us, their heads jerked around. Immediately, they let out an ear-piercing scream and turned their deformed bodies. They growled and started in our direction.

Their clothes and skin hung off of them in tatters. They groped through the air, following our smell.

From down the road, we heard a scream in the distance. Then another.

There were more coming.

Chapter 32
THE GRAVES

Old Man Miller grabbed Lauren and me by the back of our shirts and yanked us back into the house. "C'mon, get back in here quick!"

My brothers, who were deathly afraid of the house only minutes ago, darted back into the dreary hallway.

My father stood on the porch, staring at the creatures in shock, until finally Mr. Sheridan grabbed him by the arm.

"Let's go! Get back inside!" he yelled.

As soon as we were all back in, Mr. Miller slammed the door shut, just as the creatures had reached the porch steps.

"Okay, everybody, follow me quickly!" he
ordered.

We went back into the living room, and Mr.
Miller opened the hallway door at the rear of the room.

"Listen up," he said. "Here's how it goes.
Women and children, stay here. The three men, we
need to stand behind the trapdoor. Now kids, this is
very important. You have to stay quiet. If they hear
you, they won't come down to the end of the hallway to
get us. They might just break down one of these doors
and come in here."

The boys clung to my mother in the far corner of
the room, and Lauren and I stood in the back, where we
could see into the hallway. My dad came over and gave
me a kiss and told us everything was going to be all
right. And then he went and stood behind the trap.

I watched as he stood on the small ledge with
Mr. Sheridan and Old Man Miller.

"Now one of y'all has to go and unbolt the front
door," said Mr. Miller. But ya gotta hurry back here as
fast as lightning, and you have to lock the hallway door
back to the living room or the kids will be goners."

In a matter of seconds, my dad had walked back
through the living room and was at the front door. He
tried to quietly slide open the top bolt, but the creatures
reacted immediately to the slight noise.

My dad glanced back at Old Man Miller, who
urged him on. With each consecutive lock being
removed, the monsters became more enraged. The

howling and the pounding on the door grew louder by the minute. It was obvious from the sounds that there were many more than two of them right now.

My father grabbed the last lock, which was a big bolt of wood. He took a deep breath and prepared himself to sprint back down the hallway as soon as he had lifted it.

The creatures didn't wait. With a powerful burst, they broke the door off of its hinges. It sent my father hurtling backwards onto the floor.

He struggled and managed to get free from the thick, heavy door lying on top of him. He scrambled backwards like a crab with the creatures only a few feet away from him.

The first monster through the entryway tripped on the broken door lying on the floor and fell to its knees. This gave just enough time for my father to make it to his feet. He turned to run as the creatures advanced.

With them only a few feet away, there was no time to go through the living room door as planned. At a full sprint, my father ran towards the open trapdoor and attempted to leap over the gaping hole.

He landed on the other side, but not solidly, and his legs fell into the hole. He held onto the ledge with his feet dangling over the trap. Old Man Miller and Mr. Sheridan struggled to lift him up with creatures getting closer. Seeing my father in danger, I ran into the hallway and grabbed one of his arms. Finally, we were able to pull him to safety on the far ledge with the monsters just steps away.

My dad held his shin where he had hit it on the side of the trapdoor, grimacing in pain. Blood was already flowing through his pants and onto his hands. The scent of the fresh blood in the air sent the monsters into a frenzy.

Shrieking and snarling, they charged ahead towards their intended meal. The first creature lunged forward, unaware of the trap before him. He fell into the chasm but managed to grab onto the far side. It began to pull itself up, just inches away from my foot. With one hand, the monster tried to grab my ankle while trying to hold onto the ledge with the other. I pressed my back against the wall, kicking at the gruesome fingers. Then a second creature fell into the trap, landing on top of the first. Both went tumbling into the pit, howling with anger.

One by one, more creatures followed the scent of the blood and human flesh and landed into their future grave. Many more heard the howling of the monsters that had already fallen into the hole. For the next hour, howling could be heard in the distance. Closer and closer the noises became, until they found the open hallway and wandered into the open pit.

By midnight, the basement was swarming with the diseased creatures. They fought and crawled on top of each other, trying hopelessly to reach their food.

"So do we close it?" my father asked Old Man Miller.

Old Man Miller just stared down the hallway through the open door. My father reached out and grabbed his arm to get his attention.

"AHHHH! Get off me! Don't touch me!" Mr. Miller wailed to no one in particular.

He started to scratch furiously at his arms and then at the side of his face. His fingernails dug in so hard that blood began to flow down his cheek.

Old Man Miller hesitated for a moment, noticing the familiar scent of the blood. Then he looked into my eyes.

"Oh, no...it's happening to me," he said softly.

"But you didn't get your flu shots. How could that be?" I asked.

"When I was in the hospital...during the first outbreak...I did get one of them shots...but I was five...I didn't think..."

He stopped again and started digging at his eyes with his long fingernails.

"I can't...I can't see!" he screamed, covering his eyes with his bloody hands.

And then slowly, he lifted his head and stared at me. His face was pure evil. Drool ran down from his chin, and he took a step towards me as I tried to back away.

"Katie! Run away!" yelled my dad.

The sound of a voice seemed to awaken Old Man Miller into consciousness. For a moment his eyes looked normal again.

"Help me!" he pleaded.

He forced himself to turn away. And with that, he stumbled over to the open trapdoor and threw himself into the waiting hands of the infected creatures. His flesh was still healthy enough for them.

My father and Mr. Sheridan lifted the trapdoor and let it slam shut, muffling the screams from the basement.

I stepped cautiously over the closed trapdoor and walked to the still open front door at the end of the hallway to listen for other movements in the night.

After a few minutes, my dad closed the door and locked it up tight. It was safer to stay in Old Man Miller's house than to risk going back to ours while it was still dark.

We huddled together in the living room and tried to ignore the snarling and growling under the floorboards.

Chapter 33
THE GRAVES

The morning finally arrived, although without windows, we couldn't tell from inside the house. We opened the front door, and the seven of us stood on the front porch, watching and listening for signs of life.

I followed my dad up our driveway and saw that our house was undisturbed. Although it was a relief to be out of Old Man Miller's crypt, I didn't know what to expect next. Would more creatures return at night? Was it even safe in our house in the daylight?

It was decided that it was best to head out of town for a few days. We stayed outside in the open while my parents did some quick packing. Thirty minutes later, we were on the road headed towards Lauren's house to drop them off.

The roads were desolate.

We headed through the intersection and past the barber shop. We saw the library, the restaurant, and the bakery.

But I didn't see any people. Not even a single car. The place was a ghost town.

Everyone was probably at home hiding. Or maybe they had been the victims of the roaming infected. Or maybe they were creatures themselves and had burrowed themselves into a rabbit hole until dark. Either way, we weren't waiting to find out.

My dad pointed the car down Cypress Creek Road and drove a little faster than usual. Luckily, we had a full tank of gas because we were going to drive as far away as needed.

After a few miles, we turned off of Cypress Creek Road and onto State Road 2. Surely, there would be signs of life here.

I didn't know how far and how fast the virus could have spread, but we needed to find out. We had to know if this ordeal had ended or had just begun.

The farther we drove, the quieter we all became. The roads were still empty. The sidewalks were empty. All we could do was to keep driving until we saw people.

It had spread far beyond Cypress Creek. A whole lot farther.

And night was coming.

Prepare yourself for the next terrifying story coming soon from Screamin Calhoun...

The Rowan Tree

Visit Tombstonesbooks.com for more...

Made in USA - Kendallville, IN
1200702_9781530854523
12 14 2020 1401